W9-AAH-829

To Craig and Breianna
and everyone who took
time to listen to my dreams
and believe in them with me.

Sheila

To my Mom who has
supported me in my
artistic endeavors.

Kelly

Story by Sheila Sauvageau-Smestad

Cover and Illustrations by Kelly Berg

Printed by A Better Be Write Publisher
For More Information:
A Better Be Write Publisher
713 Glenside Road
Millville, NJ. 08332

Cassie's Creepy Candy Store
All Rights Reserved
Copyright ©2005 by Sheila Sauvageau-Smestad

ISBN Number 0-9767732-2-8

Printed in the U.S.A.

No part of this book may be reproduced or transmitted in any form or by any means, graphic, electronic, or mechanical, including photocopying, recording, taping, or by any information storage retrieval system, without the permission in writing by the publisher.

www.CassiesCreepyCandyStore.com

Cassie's Creepy Candy Store logo and Cassise's Creepy Candy are
Trademarks and/or Registered Trademarks of Sheila Sauvageau-Smestad

Cassie's C Creepy Candy Store ™

by Sheila Sauvageau-Smestad

illustrations by Kelly Berg

Layout, Borders, Border Illustrations, Graphic Elements
And Page Number Illustrations by Pamela Key

Cassie's Creepy Candy Store
ISBN 0-9767732-2-8
©
Copyright 2005
Sheila Sauvageau-Smestad

Printed in the U.S.A.
second printing

Hi I'm Cassie,
    welcome to my Creepy Candy Store.
Step on in;
    I will take you on a tour.

This is a candy store
that is like no other.
It even grosses out
my older brother.

6

Instead of smiley face
lollypops,
how about worm-shaped
gummy drops?

Chocolate spiders with
salty pretzel legs that sag,
if you eat them too fast,
they will make you gag!

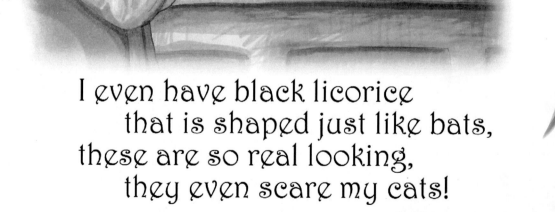

I even have black licorice
that is shaped just like bats,
these are so real looking,
they even scare my cats!

I have chocolate covered ants,
and grasshoppers too,
I just love when people gag
and then say "EWWW!"

A licorice rope
    that looks like a slithery snake,
it's so real
    it even makes me shake.

Bloody eyeballs
    that taste just like cherry,
that's the favorite
    of my best friend Mary.

Pink bubble gum
that is shaped like
little pigs feet,
oh, that is such a special
bubble-blowing treat.

White chocolate flavored
kitty cat whiskers,
they will tickle your nose,
and make you snicker.

A lot of people love
    the fudge-dipped lizard tails,
so much so
    they buy them in pails.

Wiggly and jiggly
lemon flavored frog legs,
they are a bit tart
but for more you will beg.

A featured item is my
chocolate cake
puppy dog paws,
they are so yummy
they get applause.

Mouse ears that are filled with
butterscotch cream,
so yummy, so yummy
they're like a good dream.

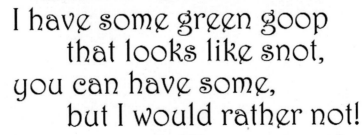

I have some green goop
that looks like snot,
you can have some,
but I would rather not!

Spider webs that are
made of cotton candy,
they melt in your mouth
and sure taste dandy.

Yellow and black bumble bees
that are filled with purple jelly,
I promise they will buzz
around in your belly.
Buzz, Buzz!

Tangerine flavored
butterfly wings,
they are so good
they will make you sing.
Laaaaaaaaaa!

Lime flavored green salamanders
filled with orange gooh,
guaranteed to ooze a lot
whenever you chew.

I have so many creepy candies,
as you can see,
next time you're in town
be sure and visit me.

Did your knees shake
    and your stomach get weak?
Just wait for my next shipment,
    it will make you freak!!

Cassie's Maze
Help get the Customers to Cassie's Candy Store

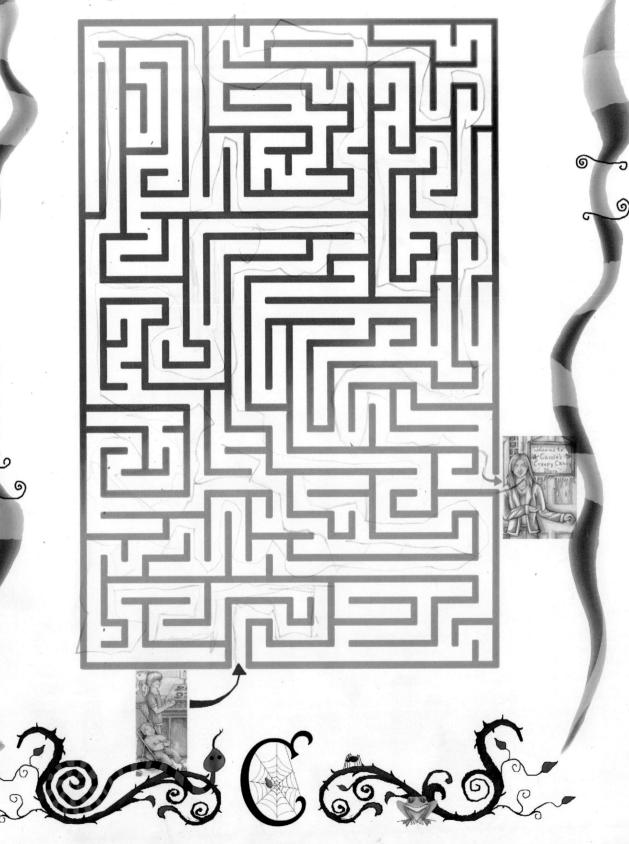

FIND THE TWINS
Find the two pictures that are identical

Cassie's Creepy Candy Store

by Sheila Sauvageau-Smestad
www.SheilaSauvageauSmestad.com

About the Author

Sheila resides in Minneapolis, Minnesota with her husband Craig and their daughter Breianna. It wasn't until the birth of Breianna that Sheila's ability to write and illustrate children's books surfaced. The joy of seeing the world through a child's eyes opened up a whole new perspective and appreciation for all that life has to offer. Sheila was able to utilize her creativity and artistic abilities to bring the world of "Cassie's Creepy Candy Store" to life. Sheila has always believed that God has blessed her with many talents. She believes the best way to thank God is to work hard and build on each one of those talents. Sheila hopes to have many children's books available for various ages of children in the near future.

About the Illustrator

Kelly Berg is an artist living in Minnetonka, Minnesota and this is her first published book as an illustrator. She is currently a student attending the Rhode Island School of Design in Providence, Rhode Island majoring in illustration. Ever since she was a child, Kelly knew she wanted to be an artist and wrote and illustrated her own books. Kelly has won many awards for her artwork including a National Portfolio Award in 2004. As a commissioned artist, she has done murals, portraits and illustrations.